Winnie's Holiday Fun

LAURA OWEN & KORKY PAUL

OXFORD
UNIVERSITY PRESS

Helping your child to read

Before they start

★ Read the back cover blurb with your child. Where do they think Winnie and Wilbur would like to go on holiday?

★ Which of the two stories does your child think sounds funniest, and why?

During reading

★ Let your child read at their own pace – don't worry if it's slow. Offer them plenty of help if they get stuck, and enjoy the story together.

★ Help them to work out words they don't know by saying each sound out loud and then blending them to say the word, e.g. *w-i-n-d-ow, window*.

★ If your child still struggles with a word, just tell them the word and move on.

★ Give them lots of praise for good reading!

After reading

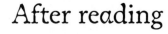

★ Look at page 48 for some fun activities.

Contents

OXFORD
UNIVERSITY PRESS

Great Clarendon Street, Oxford OX2 6DP
Oxford University Press is a department of the University of Oxford.
It furthers the University's objective of excellence in research, scholarship,
and education by publishing worldwide. Oxford is a registered trade mark
of Oxford University Press in the UK and in certain other countries

"Winnie's Wheels" was first published in *Giddy-Up, Winnie* 2009
"Winnie's Big Catch" was first published in *Winnie's Big Catch* 2009

This edition published 2020

British Library Cataloguing in Publication Data

Data available

ISBN: 978-0-19-277372-2

3 5 7 9 10 8 6 4

OX27778202

Printed in China

Paper used in the production of this book is a natural,
recyclable product made from wood grown in sustainable forests.
The manufacturing process conforms to the environmental
regulations of the country of origin.

Acknowledgements
With thanks to Caterine Baker for editorial support.

Winnie's Wheels

It was raining, and Winnie the Witch was fed up.

She watched the rain slide down the window and

sang a little song . . .

"It's raining, it's pouring,
Wilbur is snoring.
This day is very
boring, boring, boring!"

"Come on, Wilbur!" said Winnie. "Let's do something!"

But Wilbur was fast asleep – so Winnie threw a pongberry at him.

Winnie rang Jerry the giant from next door.

"Maybe Jerry can come and play with us, Wilbur."

Brrrrring! Brrrring! went the phone.

But Jerry was too busy. "Sorry, Winnie!" he said.

"I'm just off on holiday! Byeee!"

That gave Winnie a brilliant idea. "A holiday!
That's just what we need, Wilbur!"

"**Abracadabra!**" Winnie magicked
up a pile of holiday adverts.

Winnie and Wilbur looked at the adverts, but they couldn't agree where to go.

"Let's go to Africa and see the lions!" said Winnie.

"Meeow!" said Wilbur crossly. He didn't like big cats.

Then Winnie had another idea! **zing!**

"Let's go on a mystery tour!" she said. "We'll just set off and see where we end up!"

"Meeow," agreed Wilbur.

Winnie got packing.

"We need swimming costumes," she said, "and sun hats, and snow suits in case it gets cold, and some picnic food, and cooking things, and a tent, and our smelly-wellies . . ."

Winnie had a lot of suitcases. But when she put them all on the broomstick . . .

. . . it wouldn't take off!

Heave! Tug! Heave!

"We can't go for a mystery tour on a broomstick that won't fly!" said Winnie. "There's only one thing for it." She waved her wand. "**Abracadabra!**"

Suddenly, there was a beautiful, shiny car sitting in front of Winnie's house.

"That's more like it, Wilbur!" said Winnie.

Winnie began to stuff suitcases into the car boot. But soon the whole car was full.

"Gobbling goldfish, Wilbur!" said Winnie. "We still need more room! **Abracadabra!**"

A wonderful witch caravan popped up behind the car.

"Perfect!" said Winnie. "Hop in, Wilbur, and away we go!"

But Winnie didn't know how to drive. The car and caravan started going backwards, fast. Wilbur was terrified! "Meeow!"

They crashed through the stinkbushes and slimeflowers in Winnie's garden.

Thump! Bump! Thump! Bump-bump-bump.

At last they stopped in Winnie's sticky, muddy pond.

Wilbur got out of the car. His teeth chattered and his whiskers stood on end.

Winnie could see that a mystery tour wasn't a good idea.

"Let's just stay and have our holiday here, Wilbur," she said.

They quickly put the tent up. Winnie toasted some
smelly marshmallows. It was perfect!

"Meeow!" said Wilbur happily.

"We've got everything we need for a good holiday," said Winnie. "But I wish we had someone to play with."

Just then, they heard a noise.

Thud! Thud! Thud!

A big voice boomed out. "Hello, Winnie!"

It was Jerry the giant from next door and his dog, Scruff!

"I thought you were on holiday," said Winnie.

"We *are* on holiday!" said Jerry. "We put our tent up in your garden!"

So they all ate toasted smelly marshmallows and drank a big cauldron of pongberry juice.

Then they had a mud castle-building competition, using the gloopy mud from the pond.

Guess who won?

"Well, Wilbur," said Winnie later, "this is the most magical mystery tour I've ever been on!"

And Wilbur had to agree.

Winnie's Big Catch

Tomorrow was Wilbur's birthday, but Winnie hadn't got him a present yet!

"What can I get for Wilbur?" she thought. "It must be something witchy and wonderful!"

Winnie found some presents for cats on the
computer. Cat food, collars, flea powder . . .

"Boring snoring!" said Winnie. She thought and
thought. "I've got it! I won't give Wilbur a present –
I'll give him an adventure!"

Winnie looked at pictures of people parachuting, water-skiing and fishing. "Hmm," she said. "Which shall I choose? It's got to be fishing – Wilbur loves fish!"

So Winnie booked a fishing trip for the very next day.

Early next morning, Winnie and Wilbur both jumped out of bed.

"Happy birthday, Wilbur," said Winnie. "I'm taking you on a birthday fishing trip!"

Wilbur was so happy that he danced a jig, just like a sailor.

Winnie and Wilbur flew down to the seaside. They found the boat that belonged to Stinky Stan the fisherman. It was called *The Crabby Roger*.

Stinky Stan took a good, long look at Winnie and Wilbur.

"You can come in my boat," he said, "but I bet you're no good at fishing!"

"Excuse me!" said Winnie, looking cross. "Wilbur and I are both master fishermen."

Stinky Stan scratched his beard. "Are you really?"

"Yes, we are!" said Winnie. "Come on, Wilbur –
we'll show him!"

"Meeow?" said Wilbur.

So they got in the boat with
Stinky Stan.

The boat was noisy and smelly, and the waves were very big.

Up and down went the boat.

Up and down went Winnie and Wilbur's tummies.

At last the sun came out. The boat stopped bobbing up and down.

"Fiddling fish fingers!" said Winnie. "That's more like it!"

"Put some maggots on your hooks!" said Stinky Stan.

"These maggots look too good to give to the fish," said Winnie. She popped one in her mouth. Then they started fishing . . . and waited . . . and waited.

Stinky Stan pulled up fish after fish after fish.

Suddenly, Winnie felt a tug on her fishing line. "Hooray!" she yelled. "I've got a . . . washing machine. Oh dear."

So Winnie tried again. This time she got a very strange fish indeed!

"I was right!" said Stinky Stan. "You're not much good at fishing. Look at all the big fish I've got!"

"We can do better than that, can't we, Wilbur?" said Winnie. "**Abracadabra!**"

At once, Wilbur felt a

big tug on his fishing line.

They pulled and pulled. "That's not a big fish, Wilbur," said Winnie.

"It's a whale!"

Winnie and Wilbur held the rod tight. The whale pulled them super-fast across the sea.

"We're waterskiing!" yelled Winnie. "Yippee!"

"Oooer," said Stinky Stan. "Stop it! I don't like whales!"

Suddenly, there was a big gust of wind. Winnie and Wilbur flew right up in the air. **Whooooosh!**

"Wahoo!" cried Winnie. "Now we're parachuting! Isn't this fun, Wilbur?"

"Meeow!" agreed Wilbur.

At last they all got back to the shore.

"You're no good at catching fish,"
said Stinky Stan. "But you are quite
good at catching whales!"

"Tell you what," said Winnie. "Let's have a birthday barbecue on the beach. We can use those lovely fish you caught, Stinky Stan."

"All right," said Stinky Stan. "Just promise you won't invite that whale!"

After reading activities

Talk about the stories

Ask your child the following questions. Encourage them to talk about their answers.

1) In "Winnie's Wheels", why doesn't Wilbur want to go to Africa?

2) In "Winnie's Wheels", is everyone happy to have a holiday at home? What is good about it?

3) In "Winnie's Big Catch", do you think Stinky Stan changes his opinion of Winnie and Wilbur by the end? Why?

1) He doesn't like big cats; 2) Yes – there are fun things to do, nice food to eat and Jerry and Scruff are there to play with; 3) Yes, he starts off thinking they would be rubbish at fishing, but by the end he is impressed because they catch the whale.

Try this!

If you went on holiday with Winnie and Wilbur, where would you go? What would you do? Draw a picture of yourself having fun on holiday with them.

48